# The Three Bears

retold and illustrated by Kurt Nagahori

Harcourt
Orlando Boston Dallas Chicago San Diego

Visit *The Learning Site!*
**www.harcourtschool.com**

Printed in the United States of America

ISBN 0-15-314275-8

9 10 060 07 06 05